The Ten O'Clock Club

by CAROL BEACH YORK

Illustrated by
VICTORIA DE LARREA

cover by Jan Palmer

SCHOLASTIC INC.
New York Toronto London Auckland Sydney Tokyo

Other stories about the Good Day girls:

THE CHRISTMAS DOLLS
GOOD CHARLOTTE

For ELEANOR
a good clubwoman

ISBN 0-590-41084-9

Reading level is determined by using the Space Readibility Formula.
3.2 signifies high 3rd-grade level.

12 11 10 9 8 7 6 5 4 3 2 1   7 8 9 9/8 0/9

Printed in the U.S.A.   28

CONTENTS

Contents

The First Member

It was summer. In Butterfield Square the grass was green and the sun sparkled on the bright smooth leaves of the trees. All the houses around the Square seemed to turn their faces to the sun, as it shone on half-opened windows and screened doorways. Overhead a blue sky was dotted with soft clouds high up and far away, like kites freed from their strings and sailing out in space.

At Number 18 Butterfield Square, *The Good Day Orphanage for Girls,* a head appeared at an upstairs window — a head made up of two long yellow braids and a frowning face. The braids and face belonged to Elsie May, age twelve, the oldest of The Good Day girls. Right now she was looking down at the warm, peaceful summer day with a cross expression. Elsie May had decided that summer was long and hot and unexciting. Her morning chores were done. She had nothing to do until lunchtime. Life was very boring.

However, before she had sat at the window very long, a thoughtful look began to replace the frown. Maybe life was not so hopeless after all. She had an idea.

She would have a club.

In the yard below, a group of little girls sat under a tree playing. Near the top of the tree a bigger girl, about eleven years old, sat calmly across a branch. This was Kate, who could stand on her head, hold her breath the longest of any Good Day girl (in fact, until her face turned red and her eyes looked ready to pop out), and climb the highest into the old apple tree.

Elsie May did not think she would invite Kate to be in her club. Twenty-eight little girls lived at The Good Day. She would invite only the most ladylike to be members . . . she began to smile to herself as great plans for her new club grew in her mind.

She would ask Elizabeth to be a member.

And Mary.

And maybe Bonnie.

They would meet every morning at ten o'clock when their chores were done. They would be called The Ten O'Clock Club.

The meetings would last until twelve, when it was lunchtime.

They would have special projects to do.

And secret words to learn.

And secret signals. . . .

"*Kate!*" a voice demanded from the back of the house. "Get down out of that tree."

Elsie May could not actually see who spoke, but she knew it was Miss Plum's voice.

"Oh, dear, dear, dear — what will we do with you, Kate?" That was Miss Lavender, fluttery and plump. Together the two ladies, who were in charge of the twenty-eight girls at The Good Day, came walking around the side of the house. Now Elsie May could see them. Miss Plum was tall and thin, and straight as a telephone pole. Miss Lavender was short and ruffly and full of curls.

Miss Plum stood with a hand on each thin hip until Kate came down from the tree. Miss Lavender watched from over the tops of her gold-rimmed glasses, clasping her hands together because she was afraid Kate would fall.

As surefooted as a mountain goat, Kate let herself down from branch to branch, and at last dangled only a few feet from the ground. Then she dropped lightly onto the grass. Miss Lavender closed her eyes and fanned herself with relief. Miss Plum looked very serious and said, "That will be the last time I see you up so high."

"Yes, ma'am," said Kate, and ran off to find whatever else she could do that would be fun.

Elsie May moved away from her window full of disapproval for tree-climbing girls. She found some notebook paper and a pencil, and made up a pledge for her club.

I pledge to be a loyal member of the Ten O'Clock Club, and to obey its rules and keep its secrets forever and ever.

Then she went downstairs to find lady-like girls to be members of her club.

It came as quite a big surprise to Elsie May that the girls she asked to join her club said they did not want to be in a club. Or at least not in Elsie May's club — although they did not tell her that straight to her face.

"I'm too busy today," Elizabeth said.

"I'm going to play with my jump-rope," Bonnie said.

(Poor excuses, sniffed Elsie May.)

Mary said that she was writing poems and did not have time to join a club. She really was writing poems, in a yellow spiral-bound notebook.

Summer is here
The Sky is Blue
Flowers are smiling
I am too.

The real reason that Elizabeth and Bonnie and Mary didn't want to be in the club was Elsie May. She was too bossy and mean. No one wanted to be in a club with her. Elizabeth and Bonnie ran off to play, and Mary bent her red curls over her notebook.

Elsie May even asked some girls that she hadn't planned on asking, but they all said they were too busy. She even asked Kate. But Kate said she didn't like clubs.

And then she came upon Little Ann, the very smallest of all the Good Day girls. She was sitting on the slanting cellar door licking her knee where a mosquito had given her an itchy bite. To be sure, Little Ann did not look very ladylike. But Elsie May decided that she could not be so fussy after all.

"How would you like to be in my club, Little Ann?" she asked, standing by the cellar door. Little Ann was only five and wasn't sure what it meant to be in a club. But before she could ask any questions, Elsie May reached out a hand, hauled her to her feet, and carried her off to be the first member.

"You can be our vice-president," she promised.

Rules and Secret Signals

Elsie May had decided that a corner of the backyard where the handyman had put up a wooden bench against the fence would be a good place for the club meetings. And it was toward this bench that she pulled Little Ann.

"We'll have to get a table or something for the president to sit at — that's me," Elsie May explained. Little Ann did not look as if she quite understood. "That's me," Elsie May repeated, "the president. And you're the vice-president. That's the second most important thing in the whole club."

Little Ann nodded. Maybe this would not be so bad after all, she thought, although she did not like to play with Elsie May as a rule. Elsie May sometimes teased her and hid her toys. But Little Ann sat where she had been placed at one end of the bench, and Elsie May explained why she wanted to have a club.

Every morning after breakfast each girl at The Good Day had special chores to do. Some took turns helping Cook with the breakfast dishes, or helped the handyman in some way. Others dusted the parlor, or did errands for Miss Plum and Miss Lavender.

On Wednesday afternoons Miss Plum taught knitting to the girls who liked knitting. On Thursdays Miss Lavender taught sewing and embroidering to the girls who did not like knitting. And so the quiet summer days passed. Elsie May had had enough!

"Each morning at ten o'clock our club will meet here in this corner of the yard," she said carefully to Little Ann.

Little Ann nodded.

"And we will say the pledge and pay our dues and learn secret signals."

Little Ann shifted a little on the bench, but Elsie May rushed on. "Then we will greet each other with the secret handshake." She took Little Ann's hand and gave it two firm long shakes and then two quick short shakes.

Little Ann looked around, wishing someone would come along so she could get away from Elsie May.

Elsie May opened her notebook.

"Now that our first meeting has come to order with the secret handshake," she said to Little Ann, "I will write down the rules and secret signals. Your job" — she looked up from her notebook and smiled slyly at Little Ann —"will be to find some more members for the club."

"Who?" Little Ann asked.

Anyone you can get, Elsie May started to say. She stopped herself in time and

said instead, "Anyone you like, dear."

Little Ann slid down from the bench and stood staring at Elsie May's notebook. Elsie May had already headed the page *Rules* in large letters, but Little Ann could not read yet.

"Now go on, Little Ann — hurry. We need at least two more members so we can have a secretary and treasurer." Elsie May gave Little Ann an encouraging push.

"Try Tatty," she suggested. "Tatty will come, if you ask her."

Little Ann looked more sure of herself then, and trotted off in search of Tatty.

While she was gone, Elsie May continued with her list of club rules.

1. *Never be late to meetings.*
2. *Do not forget your penny each day for dues.*
3. *Learn the password and handshake and secret signals.*
4. *Do not fidget during club meetings.*
5. *Do your best at all times.*
6. *Learn the club pledge: I pledge to be a loyal member of the Ten O'Clock Club, and to obey its rules and keep its secrets forever and ever.*

When the rules were finished, Elsie May figured out the secret signals, and put them on another notebook page.

Elsie May was just finishing this when she saw Little Ann returning across the

THANK-YOU   HELLO   GOOD-BYE

HELP   YES   NO

yard. Beside her walked Tatty — and Mary, carrying her poem book.

Elsie May had to swallow her pride and accept Mary as a club member after Mary had already refused her first invitation. (Too bad — if she'd come when she was first asked, she could have been vice-president, Elsie May comforted herself.)

And Tatty, who was only seven and

always looked messy, was not what Elsie May would have hoped for in her wonderful club.

And Little Ann was only five years old!

But it seemed these were the best she could do.

The Schedule

Elsie May tried to fix Tatty by pushing her dark hair back out of her eyes and tucking in her blouse. Although Tatty somehow still did not look very neat— Elsie May said that she could be treasurer. And Mary could be secretary.

"What kind of a club is this going to be?" Mary wanted to know before she said whether or not she would be secretary. She had only come because Little Ann said she did not want to play with Elsie May all alone.

"It's going to be a very interesting club, with experiments and lots of interesting activities," Elsie May promised.

"What kind of experiments?" Mary asked.

"First let me read the rules to you," Elsie May said.

She opened her notebook and read the rules aloud, peeking up from the notebook every so often to see how the other club members were enjoying the rules, which she thought were very good.

When Elsie May had read them all, Mary said, "How come you get to make all the rules?"

Elsie May wanted to say, *Because it's my club,* but she didn't. "Would you like to add some rules?" she asked instead. She was sure she had made such complete and perfect rules that no one would be able to think of any to add.

But Mary said, "Yes, I think the rest of us should each be able to make up at least one rule of our own."

Elsie May squirmed with impatience. She was eager to get on to other things. She wanted to teach the members the pledge and the secret handshake and the secret hand signals. But she forced herself to answer as patiently as she could. "All right," she said. "You can each make up one rule." She held her pencil ready over the *Rules* page. "I'll write it down."

"Be polite," Mary said.

"Is that all — the whole rule?" (Elsie May thought that was very dumb.)

"Yes," said Mary. "Be polite."

Elsie May sighed as though this was a great effort for her, and she painfully wrote:

7. *Be polite.*

at the bottom of the list.

Next it was Tatty's turn.

"Always be careful and try not to break things if you can help it," Tatty decided.

This was even dumber than Mary's rule, Elsie May thought, but she had given up complaining since she could see that it would do no good. So she sighed again

and copied Tatty's rule after Mary's.

Little Ann could not think of any rules, so Mary helped her. "I will try to do a good deed every day," she suggested.

"This is *not* Boy Scouts," Elsie May reminded Mary. But Mary said that everybody could do a good deed a day whether they were a Boy Scout or not. So Elsie May added that rule, too.

Then Elsie May showed the other club members the pictures that she had drawn of the secret signals.

"Now we can almost talk without saying anything," she explained proudly.

Tatty and Mary practiced signaling *Hello* and *Good-bye* and *Help* to each other. Even Little Ann tried to memorize the secret signals, but when Tatty said *Hello* to her, Little Ann said *Help*, and when Mary said *Good-bye*, Little Ann said *Thank you*.

"Never mind," Elsie May said to Little Ann, "you'll learn. Every day you can practice. Now we have to choose a password, and then make up our schedule."

"How about Bluebird?" Mary suggested.

Elsie May thought that they ought to have more suggestions than just one, but Tatty and Little Ann said they thought Bluebird was fine.

"What's a password?" Little Ann whispered to Mary.

"A special word to show that you are really a true club member," Mary replied.

"But you know I am," said Little Ann.

"In case it's dark, silly," Elsie May said. Even Tatty looked at Little Ann wisely, as if to say surely Little Ann should have known *that*.

With the other things settled, it was time at last to think about their schedule. They worked very hard for a long time, sitting with heads together over Elsie May's notebook. The sun had climbed high in the sky when they were finished. The schedule looked like this:

DAILY SCHEDULE

1. *Open meeting with password and club handshake.*
2. *Treasurer will collect dues — one penny from each member.*
3. *Practice secret hand signals.*
4. *The daily experiment.*
5. *The daily walk.*
6. *End meeting by saying club pledge.*

On another page, they made a list of the experiments they would do.

EXPERIMENTS

Make cup-cakes — we will need
        eggs
        sugar
        flour
        milk

Make perfume — we will need
        dash of sugar
        water
        perfume bottles
        dash of real perfume

Plant a garden — we will need
        spoons
        seeds
        watering can

"There," said Elsie May with satisfaction. That would do for a beginning. They could think of more experiments as time went by. The schedule was perfect, and all these experiments sounded so interesting she could hardly wait to start one.

Suddenly a dark shadow fell over the page — as though some great tall dark thing had come between the girls and the sun.

Mr. Not So Much Makes
A Suggestion

The girls looked up, straight into the stern, fierce face of Mr. Not So Much, a member of the Board of Directors of The Good Day.

Once a month Mr. Not So Much came to Number 18 Butterfield Square. When he came, all the girls tried to stay out of his way, for he was always telling them, "Not so much noise," "Not so much giggling," "Not so much running." But he did not come just to tell them those things. He came to see Miss Lavender and Miss Plum about the money problems, which he felt to be out of hand. It was a tremendous problem to care for, feed, and clothe twenty-eight girls who were always growing out of their shoes, who needed school books and mittens and underwear, who seemed to be forever hungry and forever eating. When Mr. Not So Much saw The Good Day grocery bills he always said, "Not so much eating!"

And the women themselves were Mr. Not So Much's biggest problem. Miss Lavender and Miss Plum could not seem to understand Mr. Not So Much's demands for saving. They kept on in their wasteful ways. Wood burned away merrily in the fireplace in wintertime. Christmas stockings were bursting with candy and toys — *bursting!* Cook sent forth an endless stream of foods from her kitchen — cakes heaped with frosting, noodles dripping with butter, muffins stuffed with nuts and raisins. Once Mr. Not So Much had even found candied cherries in the muffins. And candied cherries were very expensive.

What could one man do against twenty-eight girls and three foolish women? He always looked as if he were about to growl. And now he appeared as frightening as ever. He towered over the small members of the Ten O'Clock Club huddled together on the handyman's bench.

"What have we here?" Mr. Not So Much asked.

Elsie May was so nervous that she let the whole notebook fall to the ground. Loose pages fluttered out, and the one entitled *Daily Schedule* landed right on Mr. Not So Much's shoe. All the girls stared at it, and watched with motionless fright as he bent and picked up the paper in his bony hands. Then he straightened stiffly like a creaking skeleton and raised the page close to his thin, stern face.

"We've having a club," Elsie May managed to say weakly. She gathered the rest of the pages and gave the whole notebook to Mr. Not So Much.

"A club, eh?" Mr. Not So Much did not

know yet whether he approved or not. He didn't know what it was going to cost.

As he read the schedule the girls had composed, it seemed plain to Mr. Not So Much that their club was not going to cost anything. It might even be a good idea.

"Very interesting," he said, looking around at the pale faces below him.

Elsie May began to look somewhat less timid. "Yes, sir," she said, "we're going to meet every morning at ten o'clock. That's our schedule for our daily activities."

"I see." Mr. Not So Much stroked his chin and his eyes narrowed thoughtfully. "When I was a boy, I belonged to a club, a club of boys who lived in my neighborhood."

Tatty and Mary looked at each other. Who knew what to think next, after such a statement? Mr. Not So Much did not look as if he could ever possibly have once been a little boy — much less the kind of boy other boys would invite to be in their club.

"Our club had a schedule, too, rather like this," Mr. Not So Much went on. "But our activities were moneymaking activities, moneymaking projects." He seemed to like the words so well that he said them again. "Moneymaking activities. Yes, indeed. Moneymaking projects. Nothing silly. Good, practical, well-thought-out moneymaking projects."

Elsie May was sorry that she had not thought of this smart idea herself. "That sounds like a good idea," she admitted.

"A very good idea," Mr. Not So Much agreed. "All the boys thought so when I suggested it."

"What moneymaking projects did you have?" Elsie May asked.

"Well, now, let me think," said Mr. Not So Much. "We shined shoes in front of the railroad station on Saturday mornings. And we did errands for the fresh fruit and vegetable grocers when they were setting up their stalls."

So far none of these things seemed

anything the girls could do. They did not know of any railroad stations or fresh fruit markets.

"And we dug worms and sold them to boys who were going fishing," Mr. Not So Much continued.

The girls' eyes widened with horror. But Mr. Not So Much did not seem to notice.

"There are any number of ways to make money," he assured them, rubbing his hands together as though even now he felt the money between his fingers. "Set yourselves to thinking. Put on your thinking caps." He tapped his own forehead firmly. "Thinking will do it, never fear."

He returned Elsie May's *Daily Schedule* page, and looked at his watch. It was time to go see Miss Plum and Miss Lavender, although he dreaded to think what wasteful ways they were up to now.

"Next time I'm here, you can let me know how much money you've made," he called to the Ten O'Clock Club as he walked off.

The girls watched him go, doubtful expressions on their faces.

What if they couldn't make any money? What would he do then?

Elsie May decided not to worry. "That was a very good suggestion, wasn't it? I'm sure there are lots of ways we can make money. It will be even more exciting than our other things."

She took a fresh page in the notebook and wrote a headline in very big letters: MONEYMAKING PROJECTS.

Nobody had any ideas for what to put next.

"I'm hungry," said Little Ann, for it was nearly lunchtime.

"So am I," said Tatty. She suddenly felt very, very hungry. She had been so busy at this club meeting, she had not been able to go around to the kitchen to visit Cook — as she usually did every morning — and see if Cook had any spare cookies or crackers.

"All right," said Elsie May. "We need time to think about some moneymaking projects. We'll end our meeting today with the secret signal for *Good-bye*, as long as you don't all know the pledge yet."

She stood up solemnly and held out her arms to make the secret signal for *Good-bye*. Tatty and Mary promptly did the same. Even Little Ann, watching the others to see what they did, managed to actually signal *Good-bye*.

"Now don't forget," Elsie May reminded everyone, "we'll meet here tomorrow at ten o'clock and think up some moneymaking projects."

Moneymaking Projects

The next morning the Ten O'Clock Club met again at the handyman's bench by the back fence. Little Ann did not have a moneymaking project to suggest, but she had learned the secret handshake and she was very proud of that. Tatty and Mary forgot that it was not fun to play with bossy Elsie May — they were so eager to begin their moneymaking projects.

"I suggest that we use our experiments for making money," Mary said, when the meeting had come to order.

Everyone else thought this was a very good idea, even Elsie May. They looked over their list of experiments and decided that their first moneymaking project would be to bake and sell their own cupcakes. They raced off to the kitchen at full speed to see Cook about how to begin.

"Cupcakes?" said Cook with a good deal of surprise. "I'm afraid I don't have any extra eggs."

"You don't?" They were all disappointed.

"Not even a tiny one?" whispered little Ann, tugging at Cook's apron and looking up hopefully.

"No," said Cook to little Ann, patting her soft yellow hair, "not even a tiny one!"

"Well," said Elsie May, "that's just fine. How can we make our cupcakes without eggs?" Cook agreed that it was a problem.

"Why do you want to make your own cupcakes?" Cook asked, as the four stood before her in a discouraged row.

"It was going to be a project for our

club to make money," Mary said.

"Oh, you have a club and you're going to make some money." Cook nodded. She thought it was all a very good idea, except, of course, there was still the problem of no eggs. Her plump face grew very thoughtful.

"How about making your own real lemonade?" she suggested after a pause. "I have everything you'd need for that, I'm sure."

"That's wonderful!" Tatty cried. "I like lemonade as much as cupcakes — don't you?" She poked Mary enthusiastically.

So Cook gave them six lemons to squeeze, and a cup of sugar, and a big glass pitcher. She also found an old card table for them to set up in the backyard. They worked very hard. When the lemonade was ready they carefully carried the pitcher out to the card table by the handyman's bench.

First came Elsie May with the pitcher.

Then came Tatty and Mary with as many

glasses as Cook said they were likely to need.

And last of all came Little Ann with a cardboard sign Elsie May had made that said:

LEMONADE
5¢ a glass

While they had been in the kitchen, two other girls, Kate and Phoebe, had come along and decided to play on the bench. Phoebe was lying with her head over the end of the bench to see if all her blood would run to her brain. Kate was just climbing from the bench to the top fence rail — where she thought she might be able to reach the lowest branch of the tree that stood there. It was hard to have a private club-meeting place in a yard that twenty-eight girls shared.

"Well!" said Elsie May in her most disgusted voice. "This is private property, in case you want to know." She came to a standstill by the card table, holding the pitcher of lemonade.

Phoebe turned her head so that her face — already an alarming shade of red — was toward them. Kate stood still in her spot on the fence.

"What's in the pitcher?" Kate asked.

"Lemonade," said Elsie May. "This is our club's meeting place, and we're going to sell lemonade. Show them the sign, Little Ann."

Little Ann came forward with the sign. Phoebe gave a last dreadful gasp and sat up straight, with tangled hair and a purple face.

Elsie May made gestures with her hands to shoo Kate and Phoebe from the bench. They stood to one side and watched as Mary and Tatty arranged the glasses around the pitcher on the card table, and Little Ann propped up the cardboard sign in the grass against one of the table legs.

"No one will see that except the grasshoppers and ants," Kate said calmly. Elsie

May looked around to see what Little Ann had done. Just then the sign fell forward into the grass, and Elsie May almost stepped on it.

"Let's put it here," said Tatty. She picked up the sign and put it on the table between two glasses. They all stood back to see how their table looked now.

"Good," said Mary with a brisk nod. "Now we're ready for business. Have you got a nickel, Kate? Phoebe?"

Kate and Phoebe were not sure that they wanted to spend a nickel on the lemonade. But as the morning passed and several other girls came by and bought lemonade, Kate and Phoebe changed their minds. They ran upstairs to their banks and each brought down a nickel.

Even the handyman, trimming the bushes at the side of the house, stopped his work long enough to have some lemonade. His face was reddened by the sun, and he was very hot and thirsty. He took two glasses and paid a dime.

"That certainly hits the spot," he said to the girls, and went back to work greatly refreshed.

All together, the Ten O'Clock Club made seventy-five cents.

"But we ought to pay Cook for the lemons and sugar," Mary said. (Elsie May was annoyed but she had to agree.) So they went back to the kitchen with the empty pitcher and the sticky glasses, and asked Cook what she thought was a fair price for the lemons and sugar that they had used.

Cook sat down at the table and thought about this carefully.

"I think the lemons should be six cents apiece," she said, "and the sugar will be fifteen cents."

That was fifty-one cents. The Ten O'Clock Club had twenty-four cents left over — twenty-four cents' profit from their first moneymaking project.

It did not seem very much after all their work.

"What we need," said Elsie May with determination, "is *something special*."

The next day they made homemade perfume and put it in empty spice bottles that Cook had in the kitchen. There were four bottles, and Cook bought one herself. Then Miss Lavender and Miss Plum each bought a bottle. When the club could not find anyone else who wanted to spend five cents for a bottle of homemade perfume, Elsie May bought the last one herself. She said that she thought it was quite a bargain and the other girls did not know what they were missing.

So then they had forty-four cents. Which was better — but not exactly earth-shattering.

"What we need," Elsie May repeated firmly, "is *something special*."

Something Special

A week passed, and no one in the Ten O'Clock Club could think of a good moneymaking project.

Every morning they followed their schedule — gave the password and handshake, collected dues, practiced secret signals, planted some flower seeds (and then inspected the ground each day to see if any flowers were coming up), and reported on their good deeds.

"I helped Cook find a button that came off her dress," Tatty reported. (Elsie May wished Tatty would pay attention to her own buttons, for the front of her dress was buttoned one button off all the way down.)

"I took a caterpillar off the steps, so nobody would walk on him and squash him," Little Ann reported.

"I helped Elizabeth put her hair in curlers," Mary said, "and I helped Miss Plum carry some books upstairs. And I helped Miss Lavender find a spool of thread that rolled under the sofa." Mary was full of good deeds.

"I'm going to braid Tatty's hair," said Elsie May. Surely this would contribute some improvement to Tatty's appearance. "That will be my good deed for today."

And they discussed ways to earn money before Mr. Not So Much returned.

"I could write poems and sell them," Mary offered.

Elsie May did not think very many people were waiting in line to buy Mary's poems.

"We could ask Kate to stand on her head and hold her breath for ten minutes, and then charge everybody a nickel to see her," Tatty suggested.

Elsie May thought that was an extremely silly idea. She didn't think anybody would pay to see Kate if she held her breath for an hour.

"If we had some glass cases, we could have a museum," Mary suggested, on another day. They did give that project some thought, and even went to ask Miss Plum if she had any glass cases they could use to make a museum. But Miss Plum did not have any.

After they talked about how to earn money, the last thing on the schedule was the daily walk. Every day they went down a different street, or off in a different direction across the Square. Elsie May always wore Cook's watch, so they would know when it was time to turn back and not be late for lunch.

And so it was that one morning, on their walk, they happened across a small, dusty-looking shop with a display of strange things in its windows. Painted on an arch over the door was the name —

There was an umbrella in the window, and a long paper snake, and lots of odd-sized boxes and painted cookie tins. The girls stood in a row, staring through the shopwindows. Then Tatty said, "Let's go in and look around."

Elsie May studied Cook's watch.

"We have twelve minutes before we have to start back," she said.

So they went to the door of the shop, and opened it and went in.

Inside everything was as dusty and jumbled and strange as the shopwindows.

The first thing they saw was a big pile of fried eggs on the counter, and half-eaten melted ice-cream bars. They stood together silently and looked at the man behind the counter. He was rather young and handsome. He pushed all the fried eggs and ice-cream bars aside, and put his arms on the counter and leaned forward to greet his customers. Then the girls saw that all the fried eggs and melting ice-cream bars were only made of plastic.

"Fool your friends?" the young man suggested, holding up a fried egg between his fingers. "Put this on the kitchen floor and somebody will go running for a mop!

"Or this —" He held up a very real-looking ice-cream bar. "This will send them running even faster."

The girls looked back and forth among themselves, giggling. What fun it would be to buy some plastic eggs and ice-cream bars and put them around to fool people.

That was not all the salesman had to show them.

"Have some cookies?" he offered, holding out a shiny red tin box. Before they could say anything, he had pulled off the cover and a great long red paper snake sprang out at them halfway across the room.

"Ohhhhhhh!" screamed Little Ann, and hid behind Mary.

Even Elsie May jumped back in fright.

Oh, if they could buy something like that. How they would surprise everybody!

Then the girls began to look around at the other things in the shop: knives that disappeared up into their own handles when they were pushed, so it looked as if you were stabbing yourself; magnetic balls that clung together in a long string; pens that fell apart when you tried to write with them; a box of rubber chocolates that really looked good enough to eat; wiggly plastic spiders; bouquets of flowers that squirted water into your face when you leaned forward to smell them.

Then, toward the back of one shelf,

Tatty saw a large round glass ball sitting apart from everything else. It was not clear glass, but cloudy and grayish-white, as though a light mist had swirled through and been caught in the glass. "What's that?" she asked the salesman, pushing the hair out of her eyes.

"Why that's a magic crystal ball," the man said.

He took it right down from the shelf and dusted it off with his handkerchief. Then he set it on the counter in front of Tatty.

"It may not look like much," he said to her mysteriously, covering it with his handkerchief. "But say the right magic words, then remove the handkerchief and look into the ball —"

By this time Elsie May and Mary had come over to stand beside Tatty and look at the magic crystal ball.

"That couldn't really work," Elsie May said. She thought the other things in the shop were much more interesting.

"Don't be so quick to turn your back on a magic crystal ball, young lady," the man said to Elsie May.

Mary was interested. She nudged Elsie May and drew her aside. "Even if it didn't really work," she said, "we could pretend it did. We could use it for a moneymaking project, telling everybody's fortune."

Elsie May looked over her shoulder at the crystal ball. The salesman had covered it with his handkerchief again. He was showing Tatty how to pull off the handkerchief with a mysterious flourish and then gaze into the wonderful crystal ball.

"You might have something," Elsie May admitted slowly, turning back to Mary. "We could tell fortunes. We could charge a nickel a fortune — no, a dime. But I wonder how much the ball costs."

"Let's ask," Mary said. "We have fifty-six cents in our treasury, not counting our dues."

They went up to the counter again, and Elsie May said, "Excuse me, but how much do you want for that old glass ball?"

The salesman smiled. "This old glass ball," he repeated in a mocking tone. "Please, ladies, this is a genuine magic crystal ball. Stare into its glowing depths, see the future right before your eyes."

How exciting to have discovered a magic crystal ball, thought Tatty. "Oh, let's buy it, let's buy it," she said to Elsie May.

Elsie May, in her most businesslike manner repeated her question. "How much does it cost?"

"A dollar," the salesman replied, checking a pencil mark on the bottom of the base. "And a bargain at any price, ladies."

"A dollar?" Mary echoed with disappointment.

Elsie May was disappointed too, but she drew herself up and said, "A dollar — for just a plain old glass ball? This cookie box with the snake is more exciting than that, and I see it's marked only fifty cents."

"Do you want the cookie box instead?" The salesman set down the crystal ball and held out the candy box.

"Oh, no, no," Tatty said. Mary and Elsie May whispered with their backs turned. At last Elsie May was ready. "We could give you fifty cents for the crystal ball," she offered.

The salesman did not answer at once. At last he said, "Well, I'll tell you, ladies, as long as you seem to like it so much I think I could see my way clear to knocking off the price a little."

They were surprised and overjoyed to have everything settled so quickly. Why, the salesman had not argued at all. Surely the crystal ball was meant to be theirs.

Elsie May remembered the time suddenly and looked at her watch. "Oh — our twelve minutes are up. We have to get right back for lunch. We don't have any money with us now, anyway. Will you keep the crystal ball for us until tomorrow? We can come back tomorrow morning and bring you the money."

"Fair enough," said the salesman.

"Don't sell it to anyone else," Tatty begged.

"I won't," the salesman promised.

Tatty, Elsie May, and Mary looked at each other, smiling. Here was their *something special*.

They found Little Ann behind a display of umbrellas that were full of holes when they were opened up, and they all rushed away together toward Butterfield Square and lunch.

They had found their *something special*. And tomorrow it would be theirs.

A Surprise for Cook

The next morning the Ten O'Clock Club members got right down to the business of going to buy the crystal ball. They skipped over all the other parts of their meeting, including the handshake, and password, and secret signals — to the great relief of Little Ann, who had forgotten them all again. They jumped over their whole list of rules and schedule down to "daily walk," and set out for the Palace of Magic at once.

Tatty, as treasurer, was in charge of the money. She proudly carried the little purse containing the club's fifty cents.

Everything at the shop was just the same. Dusty and jumbled, full of wiggly plastic spiders and melting ice-cream bars, trick knives, and snakes in candy boxes. The salesman was glad to see them. He got up from a stool where he had been sitting and took down the crystal ball from the shelf behind the counter where he had put it to save for them.

Slowly he counted the fifty cents. Then he put the crystal ball into a large paper bag and handed it across the counter.

Elsie May thanked the man for keeping the crystal ball for them. Then, as club president, founder, and oldest member, she felt that it was her right to carry the paper bag. The others trailed after her out of the Palace of Magic, along the street toward Butterfield Square and The Good Day. They were all filled with excitement and anticipation.

"First we'll have to make a big sign," Elsie May explained as they hurried along. She had been very busy thinking about their fortune-telling business. "And we must have the right costumes to wear — you know, long dresses and maybe some big earrings, like gypsies."

"Let's try it out on somebody first," Tatty begged. She didn't think she could wait the long time for Elsie May to make a sign and find some costumes and all *that!*

"We could give Cook a free fortune," Mary said with inspiration. As they drew near the back door they could see Cook standing by the open screen shaking crumbs from a tablecloth.

"Oh, let's — please, Elsie May," Tatty pleaded.

"Well, all right," Elsie May agreed. "I guess that wouldn't hurt."

Cook had gone back into the kitchen. As the club members came through the door she was sitting with her back to them at her worktable reading a recipe book. She was so absorbed in the ingredients for gingerbread with lemon sauce that she jumped with surprise when she heard the screen door close. At the same moment she felt Elsie May tap her shoulder.

"What — oh —" Cook started up and then sank back with relief. "You children startled me. What have you got there?" She was watching as Elsie May gently set down her brown bag and carefully took out the precious crystal ball. "What's that?" asked Cook. "A paperweight?"

"Pretty big for a paperweight," Elsie May said wisely. "This is a fortune-telling crystal ball, and we want to see —"

"We want to see if it works," Tatty interrupted eagerly. "We want to read your fortune."

Cook smiled at Tatty, who stood with hair straggling into her eyes and several spots of unknown substance on the front of her dress.

"All right," said Cook. She pushed away her recipe book and turned her attention to the large ball on the table. The bottom of the ball was flat, so it rested nicely wherever it was put and did not roll away.

"Make it a good fortune, now," Cook urged.

"I will tell just what it says," Elsie May replied coolly.

"We need a handkerchief," Mary reminded Elsie May in a loud whisper.

There did not seem to be a handkerchief among the four of them, so Cook gave them a napkin from a stack on the table. Elsie May laid it over the crystal ball with great ceremony.

Everyone waited with breathless silence as Elsie May slowly pulled away the napkin, meanwhile repeating the words that the salesman had taught them:

"Mystic ball, tell me all.
Reveal your secrets
and let me see the time beyond."

Cook blinked and drew back a little, and Little Ann felt a shiver run from the top of her head to the tip of her toes. Tatty and Mary leaned against the table so hard that Elsie May had to stop fortune-telling

long enough to say, "You are knocking the
table over."

Tatty and Mary drew back quickly, and
waited more impatiently and more excit-
edly than ever for Elsie May to continue.

Slowly Elsie May drew her fingers across
the surface of the ball. Then she put her
face down close to it and squinted into
the cloudy glass. "I see someone standing

by a door . . . yes, yes, it's Cook — standing by a door . . . Oh, I do, I really do see her! I really, really do!" Elsie May leaned closer to the ball, her face radiant with delight and surprise.

"Oh — go on — go on!" Tatty and Mary did not know what else to do so they hugged each other and jumped up and down.

Cook covered her mouth politely with her hand so the girls would not see that she was trying not to laugh.

"Yes — yes." Elsie May was now so excited she could barely talk. "Someone is coming to the door and handing something to Cook. It's — it's —" She squinted harder and harder into the cloudy glass. "— It's a letter — some kind of a special letter, for Cook is very happy and kisses the envelope and presses it to her heart!"

Just then a knock at the screen door broke the spell of the circle around the kitchen table. They all turned to see Mrs. Cummings, who lived in a house across the Square. She held her hand over her eyes to see in through the screen. Cook got up and went to the door.

"Hello, Mrs. Cummings," Cook said. She pushed open the screen. "Come in."

"I can't stay," Mrs. Cummings replied. "I just ran over with this. The mailman left it at my house by mistake." She handed Cook a white envelope, and looked past her into the kitchen where the Ten O'Clock Club stood at the table. "Hello there, girls," she called to them. "Well, I must be getting back home." She waved once more and tripped away.

"Why, it's a letter from my sister. I was just thinking about her yesterday and wishing I'd hear from her." Cook kissed the envelope and pressed it close to her heart — *and then she realized what she was doing.*

"Why — why —" She spun around and stared at the four girls at the table. Their eyes were as round as dinner plates, and so were their mouths. But only for a moment were they silent.

"It works — it really works!" Tatty shouted, and Mary began to hug Tatty and shout, too. "It really works — oh, think of the money we'll make now."

"I saw it, I really saw it." Elsie May wanted everybody to listen to her, but they were all talking at once.

"My turn, my turn," Little Ann was saying. And when at last they could gather themselves together enough to hurry off with their magic crystal ball, Little Ann was still begging, "My turn, my turn," as she ran after them.

When the girls were gone, Cook sat down thoughtfully at her kitchen table again. She opened the letter from her sister, and as she smoothed the pages and began to read she was thinking, "Well, this was only a coincidence, the letter coming at just this moment. I hope the girls don't make too much of it."

A Busy Afternoon

The members of the Ten O'Clock Club spent all that afternoon getting ready to be fortune-tellers. They planned to start telling fortunes promptly at ten o'clock the next morning, as soon as they had said the password and greeted each other with the secret handshake. They were going to skip the report on good deeds and the daily walk and the daily experiment — no flowers were yet in sight, so that was not very much fun anyway.

They prepared a large sign, beautifully colored with Mary's crayons and stuck all over with gold-star stickers donated by Miss Lavender.

Miss Plum gave them a large turban hat made of blue velvet. "I was saving it until the style came back," Miss Plum said, "but it doesn't seem to be coming back."

Miss Lavender gave them a large feathery fan and a real-silk handerchief. Then she set aside less interesting sewing (like mending socks and letting down hems) and fixed up several of her old dresses into long gypsy costumes. She even found the fortune-tellers some earrings to wear, and said they could use her rouge to make their cheeks red.

Elsie May was to have the turban. She put her long braids on top of her head and clapped the turban down over them.

Mary was to have the feather fan to hold. She was also to be in charge of the handkerchief.

Tatty was to collect the money, and she had an empty candy box shaped like a heart.

And Little Ann was to carry the sign:

FORTUNES TOLD
10¢
Gypsies look deep into your future
and reveal secrets of the
time to come.

They decided to charge ten cents a
fortune, now that they knew their crystal
ball really worked.

"Ten cents," Mary muttered as she
carefully colored in the letters of the sign.
"We ought to charge about a dollar."

"Except nobody could come then," Tatty
reminded her. None of the girls at The
Good Day had a dollar to spare for
anything, even a view of their future.

But Miss Plum and Miss Lavender
wondered if even ten cents might be
asking too much.

"Are you sure you'll have any customers
at that price?" Miss Plum said, when they
brought their sign to show her.

"Ten cents isn't much for a real true fortune," Elsie May said.

"I had mine free of charge," Cook said, walking into the parlor at just that moment with the afternoon tea.

"Yes, indeed," Cook went on, as Miss Plum and Miss Lavender listened with polite interest. "This very morning. I believe it was the first fortune of all."

"It was," said Tatty. "It was a wonderful fortune."

"It certainly was." Cook winked at Miss Plum and Miss Lavender, but she was careful the girls did not see. "I'd been wishing I would hear from my sister, it had been so long since she'd written to me. And then in the crystal ball Elsie May saw a letter coming for me — and hardly a minute later there was a letter from my sister."

Cook had the letter in her apron pocket even then and she took it out, to the great delight of Tatty, Mary, Elsie May, and Little Ann.

"My, my." Miss Plum winked back at Cook. They knew it was all a coincidence.

Miss Lavender was somewhat more impressed, however. "Isn't that something!" she exclaimed. She took Little Ann on her lap and kissed her round warm pink cheek and smoothed back her fine yellow hair. "And what do you think of all this?" she asked Little Ann.

"I'm going to carry the sign," Little Ann replied. But she was really rather worn out from all the excitement of the day. She snuggled down in Miss Lavender's lap and went to sleep.

Leaving Little Ann behind, the other club members went outside to their bench to continue plans for the next morning's activities.

"I think we ought to take turns telling the fortunes," Mary said.

"So do I," Tatty agreed quickly. She didn't see why Elsie May should have all the fun.

Elsie May thought this was an extremely dumb idea.

"I'm the oldest," she reminded them firmly. "And I started the whole club. And I'm the president."

"But I found the crystal ball," Tatty reminder her.

"And I thought of using it for a money-making project," Mary said.

Finally, Elsie May had to give in. They would take turns telling fortunes. She supposed that was the way things went when you had a club — everybody wanted a turn at everything.

Fortunes — 10¢

The next morning the very first paying customer for the gypsy fortune-tellers was Kate. She was swinging from the tree branch over the handyman's bench when the Ten O'Clock Club arrived for the opening of their meeting.

Kate was so surprised at what she saw that she plunked right down to the fence, then to the bench, then to the ground.

"What are *you* dressed up for?" Kate asked in amazement. She stared at Elsie May in her turban and some of Miss Lavender's rouge; at Tatty carrying a heart-shaped candy box; at Little Ann with silver earrings and a star-covered sign; and at Mary strutting along like a queen fluttering her fan.

"We are gypsy fortune-tellers, if you don't mind," Elsie May explained. She held out the crystal ball for Kate to see. "If you have ten cents you may have your fortune told in our marvelous crystal ball."

"Ha, ha," said Kate.

"But it really works, Kate," Tatty said. "We told Cook's fortune and it came true."

"Naturally," Elsie May remarked.

"Naturally," Mary agreed from behind the fan.

Kate began to be curious. "How does it work?" she asked.

"You can't find out without a dime," said Elsie May. "Now if you will excuse me, our meeting must come to order."

She shooed Kate away, but Kate did not go far. She stood aside just enough to suit the Ten O'Clock Club, and no farther. She could not hear what they said, but she saw that they all did something with their hands, even Little Ann. But what Little Ann did wasn't much like what the others did. Then there was some discussion around Little Ann. At last the club members sat down in a row on the bench with the crystal ball on the card table in front of them, ready for business.

Suddenly Kate dashed away. When she came back, she had not only brought ten cents for her fortune, but she had also brought Phoebe and Jane. They had each brought a dime, just in case. They were going to wait first, and see what the fortune-telling business was like before they spent their money.

"Ahhh," said Elsie May, trying to sound like an old gypsy lady, "whom do we have here? Someone who would like a fortune told? Come closer, closer." She tried to make her voice mysterious. Phoebe and Jane began to giggle. But all the club members looked so serious that Phoebe and Jane stopped giggling and came close behind Kate as she laid her ten cents down on the table. They didn't want to miss anything.

Elsie May covered the crystal ball with the beautiful real-silk handkerchief. *"Mystic ball, tell me all,"* she whispered dramatically. *"Reveal your secrets and let me see the time beyond."* Little Ann felt the shivers going down her back again. Tatty squeezed Mary's hand so tightly that Mary nearly cried out.

Then Elsie May drew off the handkerchief. Beneath stood the grayish glass, clouds swirling inside. Kate and Phoebe and Jane all leaned closer.

"I see Kate going along a street . . ." Elsie May looked deep into the crystal ball. "Why, it looks like our street, right here in the Square — yes, I can see our fence. And there's Kate going along on her skates, smiling and waving to everyone."

"That's not me," said Kate, shaking her head. "I can only find one skate. I've been looking all week for the other."

Elsie May thought how like Kate it was to lose a skate. But she saw what she saw. "It's you," she insisted. "Ah — now the vision is fading." Elsie May leaned closer to the ball. "Everything is gone. I don't see anything more."

There was a silence. Everyone waited for Elsie May to say something else. At last she said, "Well, that's your fortune — don't blame me."

"Some fortune," said Kate.

"Can't you see anything else for her?" Tatty whispered anxiously.

Elsie May stared into the ball again, but she could see nothing more.

"What a gyp," Kate said. "I ought to get my money back."

"Now, that's not fair." Mary looked out quickly from behind her fan, her red curls bouncing. "You wanted your fortune told, and we told it. You have to be patient. Every fortune can't come true in an instant."

Kate looked very annoyed. She thought she would rather have her dime for candy than a silly old fortune.

"Come on, Phoebe, how about you?" Mary said cheerily, trying to ignore Kate. "Come on, have your fortune told."

Phoebe did not look very eager to part with her dime, and Jane shook her head and said Kate was right and it was a big gyp.

Just then Miss Plum's voice came clearly across the yard from the kitchen door.

"Kate — Kate — I've found that skate you were looking for — " They could see Miss Plum standing there in the doorway, holding a skate in her hand.

"I think maybe I will have my fortune told after all," said Phoebe, as Kate sprinted away toward the back door to get her skate. Kate was soon telling Miss Plum in a jumble of words about Elsie May telling her fortune. And Cook came to the door and stood beside Miss Plum.

Miss Plum smiled and shook her head in surprise. "My, my," she said. "Is that so?" She was glad to see that the girls were having so much fun.

Cook told Kate about her fortune — about the letter that had come from her sister. Oh, it was only a coincidence, Cook knew — and she winked at Miss Plum. But after Miss Plum had gone back to the parlor and Kate had gone back to the bench to listen to the fortune-telling, Cook stood a few moments at the kitchen door, watching the girls gathered around the rickety old card table . . . and she was not so sure what she thought now, after all.

Miss Plum's Decision

For the next few mornings the Ten O'Clock Club was very busy telling fortunes. Every little girl at The Good Day had her fortune told at least one time, and in between fortunes they sat in the grass around the card table and talked about gypsies and crystal balls. Mary let them feel the silky feathers of her feather fan.

All the fortunes came true. Every one. Some almost right away, others before the day was over. The fortune that took longest to come true was Bonnie's.

It had been Mary's turn to tell the

fortune, and she looked into the crystal ball and saw something small and furry in Bonnie's arms. Was it a puppy or a kitten? Mary could not be sure.

All afternoon the girls hunted around the yard. No puppies or kittens appeared. Some of the girls were beginning to wonder if the crystal ball still worked. They were just about ready to give up when they heard Bonnie gasp. Something had fallen out of a tree and right into her arms — something small and furry.

"My teddy bear!" Kate cried. "I must have left him up there this morning."

Of course, reports of these activities reached Miss Plum and Miss Lavender. One morning when the Ten O'Clock Club was coming in to get ready for lunch, Miss Lavender stopped them in the hall outside the parlor door.

"How would you like to tell my fortune in your crystal ball?" she said.

"Oh, that would be fun," Tatty said.

"Let me, Elsie May. It was going to be my turn next when we stopped."

"All right," Elsie May said — not very happily. She would have liked to tell Miss Lavender's fortune herself.

Carrying the crystal ball, Elsie May went into the parlor, followed by Mary with the fan, Tatty with the collection box, and Little Ann with the sign.

Miss Plum was sitting at her desk, getting the month's bills in order before Mr. Not So Much's next visit. She looked up with surprise to see the strange parade in their long bright skirts coming through the door.

"Why don't you put your crystal ball on this table by the sofa, Elsie May?" Miss Lavender suggested. "Now we can all sit here together and see what Tatty can find out for my fortune."

They all sat in a line on the sofa, Little Ann in Miss Lavender's lap. Tatty bent over the table and peered into the ball.

Clearer and clearer in the swirling mists of the crystal ball Tatty saw Miss Lavender sitting on the sofa. Miss Lavender was all alone — but then she reached up her hand as though she was taking something from somebody, and then she began to smile.

"I see you, I see you," Tatty began.

"You're sitting on the sofa, and someone is giving you something . . . oh, it's a pair of earrings. You're putting them on. A beautiful new pair of earrings . . . you're going to look in the mirror . . ." And as Tatty watched, Miss Lavender's vision disappeared into the mists of the crystal ball, and only the white clouds remained.

"How exciting," Miss Lavender declared. "Isn't that exciting, Little Ann?"

"You have to wait, you know," Elsie May reminded Miss Lavender. "Some of the fortunes don't come true right away."

"Bonnie had to wait a long time," Little Ann whispered in Miss Lavender's ear.

"I see." Miss Lavender nodded wisely.

"I've written a poem about that," Mary told Miss Lavender.

"Have you?" Miss Lavender was quite impressed.

Knowing it by heart, Mary was pleased to say her poem for Miss Lavender.

"Whether it's soon
Or whether it's late
Your fortune by noon
Or your fortune by eight —

Your fortune by nine
Or your fortune by two
Just given time
It's sure to come true."

"That's a wonderful poem, Mary," Miss Lavender said.

Tatty had gone over to Miss Plum's desk and stood close to her elbow, until Miss Plum noticed her and looked up.

"Can I tell your fortune, Miss Plum?" Tatty asked. But just then they all heard the clock striking twelve. It was lunchtime, and the girls were not out of their fortune-telling costumes. Their hands were not washed. Their hair was not combed. Little Ann did not have any shoes and socks on.

"Hurry now, girls," Miss Plum said kindly, setting aside her own work when she heard the clock striking. "Perhaps you may tell my fortune another time."

The girls scrambled off, holding up their long skirts, Elsie May's turban slipping over one eye.

Miss Plum shook her head and laughed as she stood up from the desk. She had been listening to Miss Lavender's fortune, and now she said, "You won't believe this, Miss Lavender, but I came across this pretty pair of earrings when I was straightening my bureau drawer the other day — they're much more your style than mine. I've been meaning to give them to you and I keep forgetting."

She had taken the earrings from the desk and now handed them to Miss Lavender, who could only shake her head in wonder. Then she had to put on the earrings and go to the mirror by the desk to see how they looked.

"It's amazing, isn't it, Miss Plum?" Miss

Lavender said, as she turned her head from side to side.

Miss Plum did not answer at once. She stood thoughtfully, watching Miss Lavender. Then at last she said very seriously, "I think the time has come, Miss Lavender, for us to find out a little more about this crystal ball. I think the time has come for us to pay a visit to that — what was the name of that shop?"

"The Palace of Magic," Miss Lavender said.

"Yes," Miss Plum said, "of course. The Palace of Magic. Yes, I think the time has come to pay a visit there."

The Palace of Magic

The first opportunity for Miss Plum and Miss Lavender to visit The Palace of Magic came the next morning. Right after breakfast they set out together without a word to anyone.

They went down the walk, out of the gate, and across the Square.

Woolcott Street seemed the best place to look. There were many little shops there, so they turned in that direction. It did not take long to reach Woolcott Street, and there, sure enough, was the small dusty shopwindow and the letters —

THE PALACE OF MAGIC

"Some Palace," Miss Plum remarked under her breath. She could not stand dust or clutter. And she had just caught sight of some plastic spiders in one corner of the window.

"Do you think we should go in?" Miss Lavender asked doubtfully. She knew she would not touch anything in there.

"That's what we came for," Miss Plum said, and boldly opened the shop door. Miss Lavender shivered a little, but she followed Miss Plum.

They stood inside the door, getting their bearings in the dimly lit shop. At that hour of the morning the sun did not come in from the street. Behind the counter the salesman got up from his stool and leaned forward in a friendly way, just as he had done for the members of the Ten O'Clock Club.

"What can I do for you lovely ladies this morning?" he began cheerfully. Miss Plum sniffed with disapproval at the words "lovely ladies." She was always suspicious of flattery. Miss Lavender, however, gave the man a small smile.

"We've heard about your shop," Miss Plum began, choosing her words carefully. She looked around sharply as she spoke, however. She intended to find out what she could before she mentioned the crystal ball.

"Cookies, ladies?" The man held out a brightly painted tin. Before they could answer he lifted the lid politely. Out sprang the long red paper snake —

straight into Miss Plum's face. She jumped, clutching her purse tightly.

"Oh, my, my, my!" Miss Lavender was startled, too. "Oh, how my heart is going pitter-patter!" she exclaimed.

"Well." Miss Plum straightened her hat, and stood eyeing the young man with disapproval. "I hope that is the extent of your tricks."

"Oh, ladies, please — a little joke." The salesman tucked the paper snake back into the candy tin. "I didn't think it would scare you so much."

"Hmmm," said Miss Plum.

"Let me show you some of my other things. I know you'll find something you like. A fried egg perhaps? Fool your friends. Just put one under the table or in the middle of the kitchen floor. No? Well, how about a trick pen? Falls all apart and squirts you with water on top of that. No? How about this drinking glass . . ."

He opened up bunches of trick flowers. He showed them long chains of steel loops

that fell apart when he shook them a certain way. Rings with secret compartments. The umbrellas with holes . . . and on and on. Miss Lavender became interested in spite of herself — although she remembered not to touch anything. Miss Plum stood sternly by and shook her head over such foolishness.

At last, Miss Plum said, "What we really came for was to inquire about a crystal ball which you sold to some little girls not long ago."

"The crystal ball? Sure, I remember that. Marvelous thing, that crystal ball." He winked at Miss Plum, who leaned forward somewhat stiffly and said, "What do you mean 'marvelous'?"

The shopkeeper shrugged. "You know — just a joke. I told the little girls that if they said certain magic words and waved a handkerchief around — you know, a lot of hocus-pocus — they could tell the future. They thought it was great."

"I know." Miss Plum continued to study

the salesman intently. She wanted to decide whether he was trying to fool her or not. Then she said, "But you didn't really believe there was anything unusual about the ball, did you?"

The salesman looked somewhat sheepish. "No, of course not. I just said that for the little girls." Then he added quickly, "But all my other things really work." He began opening paper flowers and holding out collapsing pens.

"Wait, wait, please." Miss Plum held up a hand. "I'm really not interested in buying anything. I just wanted to know about the crystal ball."

The salesman shrugged again. "There's not anything to know. It was probably the only thing I had that was a real fake."

"Where did you get it?" Miss Plum asked.

The salesman frowned and studied the ceiling. "Why, I guess I didn't get it anywhere, now that I think of it," he said. "It was just left here along with some other odds and ends when I bought the shop."

"Has it always been a — " Miss Plum halted for lack of the right word. At last, not being able to think of anything better, said, "Has it always been a 'Palace of Magic'?"

"Yes," the young man replied. "Far as I know. I didn't change the name when I came. Just bought out the old owner and took over."

"Who was the former owner?" Miss Plum asked next.

"Old guy name of Perkins. He moved away."

Well, that seemed to be the end of that. Neither Miss Plum nor Miss Lavender could think of anything more to ask. Old Mr. Perkins had sold his Palace of Magic to this young man, and the glass ball had been gathering dust on the shelf there ever since. Until Elsie May, Tatty, Mary, and Little Ann had carried it off to Butterfield Square.

"Did you ever have any other crystal balls?" Miss Plum asked this one last question as she prepared to leave.

"Nope, I never did," the salesman said. "It was the only one. Anyway," he went on carefully, "what's the difference? A plain glass ball, that's all it was, honest. If the little girls had some fun with it, isn't that enough? There wasn't anything magic about it."

Miss Plum paused with her hand on the doorknob. "I'm not so sure, young man," she said.

"Quite a few fortunes have come true," Miss Lavender added over her shoulder. She followed Miss Plum outside.

As they went off along the street, the salesman kept his eyes on them.

He had seen a lot of nutty things in his time — but these two ladies were the nuttiest of all!

Elsie May's Fortune

At about the same time that Miss Plum and Miss Lavender were bidding good-bye to the man at The Palace of Magic, the Ten O'Clock Club was preparing for the business of the day: reading fortunes. But on this morning they began by moving the card table out by the front walk, under the trees. Elsie May said that would be a better location in case any passersby wanted their fortunes told.

The club had thought of going outside the gate, but Cook had said she did not think Miss Plum and Miss Lavender would approve of that.

However, Elsie May felt they were close enough to the sidewalk for anyone going by to see them and their crystal ball and their sign.

What they needed were new customers. For it seemed that at last they had collected every cent they could from The Good Day girls. Dimes were not easy to come by, and many girls had already given up an afternoon's ice-cream cone to have their fortune read. The treasury of the Ten O'Clock Club was bulging. Tatty, the treasurer, counted it once at three dollars and sixty cents, and once at three dollars and seventy cents, and one time she had even counted it as high as three dollars and eighty-five cents.

While they waited for some passersby to come along, the club members practiced their secret hand signals. But when Kate and Phoebe came strolling by looking for something to do, Elsie May said that they had better stop their secret signals. It was not long before other girls began to drift out of the house and gather around the crystal ball on the card table. Even without a dime to have a fortune told, it was fun to watch other fortunes come true.

The Square was very quiet that morning. It was a hot day. No one seemed to be out.

"I know what," Elsie May decided at last, when there was no sign of any business at all. "I think I will have my fortune told."

"Oh, good!" said Mary.

"My turn," said Little Ann, but Little Ann did not always tell things right, so Elsie May said that she would rather have Tatty tell her fortune. (Actually, Elsie May felt that no one told fortunes as well as she did herself, but you couldn't tell your own fortune.)

Tatty said the magic words and stared into the crystal ball. For a long time she did not see anything except the swirling grayish streaks in the glass. Then at last she began to see something glittering and sparkling. Then, slowly, but ever more clearly, she began to see someone in the crystal ball.

"I see you, I see you," she announced to Elsie May.

"Yes? Yes?" Elsie May urged her on.

"You're wearing your turban — and

there are all kinds of little sparkling things around you — "

"Diamonds!" Mary exclaimed, fanning herself with excitement.

"Diamonds!" echoed Elsie May. She personally thought that she deserved nothing less.

"I can't tell if they're diamonds or not." Tatty squinted at the ball, and then began to shake her head. "I guess it couldn't be diamonds," she said, "because you don't look very happy."

"I don't?" said Elsie May.

"You look very surprised — and — " Tatty hesitated. " — and sort of angry."

"Are you sure it's not diamonds?" Elsie May leaned forward and tried to see into the crystal ball herself. And just then Kate hung down by her knees from a low tree branch and tickled Phoebe with the leafy end of a tiny twig she had pulled off. Phoebe had been listening to Elsie May's fortune, and the sudden soft tickle on her ear frightened her. She swatted at her ear and whirled around so fast she hit the card table. It tipped over and the crystal ball fell to the sidewalk and smashed into a hundred sparkling pieces.

After a stunned moment of silence when nobody spoke or moved, Elsie May was the first to find her voice.

"Phoebe!" she screamed, close to tears. "You are as clumsy as a COW!"

The other girls could only look. There lay the wonderful, marvelous, crystal ball. Broken beyond repair. Its mysteries and its magic gone forever.

The Last Meeting

As Miss Plum and Miss Lavender came through the front gate, they could tell that something was wrong. All the girls seemed to spring at them at once, each trying to tell what had happened in her own way.

It was a great confusion to the women, as Elsie May's diamonds, a cow, and a crystal ball all rolled together in one strange story. But then at last, when Miss Plum held up her hands to beg for silence, it became clear that the crystal ball was broken.

Miss Plum and Miss Lavender's first impression was a feeling of relief but then they saw at once that it was quite a tragedy to the girls.

"Now, now, don't cry, Tatty, don't cry, Little Ann," Miss Lavender soothed, trying to wipe off their warm wet little faces with her handkerchief. "It's not as bad as all that."

When the girls were reasonably quiet, Miss Plum said comfortingly: "Think of it this way. You've all had a lot of fun with the crystal ball, and perhaps it is for the best this way — "

"Best? Best?" the girls all cried out at once. How could Miss Plum say that, they wondered.

"Yes, for the best," Miss Plum repeated. "After all, Elsie May, I think your club has made about all the money they can make telling fortunes here. The girls can't have much left to spend on fortunes."

"We could have gone out into the world," Elsie May protested sadly. "We could have told fortunes to other people."

"I'm afraid not, dear," Miss Plum replied

gently. "Have you forgotten school will be starting week after next?

"And, anyway," Miss Plum concluded, "isn't it really better to take things as they come, to do our best every day and not be worrying and wondering what's going to happen in the future?"

The girls did not seem to think anything made up for breaking the marvelous, magic crystal ball, but they set about making the best of what had happened. Phoebe and Kate said they were sorry for their part in breaking the crystal ball, and everyone helped clean up the pieces of glass on the walk.

The next morning the Ten O'Clock Club had its last meeting. They opened the meeting by saying the password, giving the secret club handshake, and saying *Hello* with the secret hand signal.

They counted all the money they had made by telling fortunes and paying dues, and it came to three dollars and ninety-two cents — ninety-eight cents each.

"I'm going to buy all the candy I can eat," Mary announced. "And maybe I'll spend fifty-nine cents for a new poem book."

"I'm going to buy all the candy I can eat, too," Tatty decided.

"Me, too," said Little Ann, "Ice-cream cones and candy."

"I'm going to save mine and buy a fur coat when I grow up," Elsie May said. They all looked at her with admiration. They had long ago forgotten that it was not much fun to play with her.

"Can we have a club again next summer?" Mary asked eagerly.

"I don't see why not," said Elsie May. "Maybe by then some of the members will be better able to learn their secret hand signals." And she looked straight at Little Ann, who did not notice because she had spotted a caterpillar crawling through the grass and had knelt down to watch it. She did not hear what Elsie May was saying, or that all of a sudden Elsie

May stopped talking and it got very quiet.

Little Ann was crawling along in the grass after the furry caterpillar, when she came to a pair of large black shoes. They were attached to a pair of long black trousers that were attached to a white shirt and black coat . . . that were attached to the long, thin, fierce face of Mr. Not So Much.

Little Ann looked up, up, up into that face, which seemed to hang in the sky above her.

"How is the club coming along?" Mr. Not So Much asked, stepping carefully around Little Ann and the caterpillar.

The other girls, who had grown quiet at his approach, looked up at him timidly.

"We've had lots of moneymaking projects," Mary began, and then Tatty and Elsie May took up the story, too. They all wanted Mr. Not So Much to hear about the crystal ball, and they showed him the four little piles of dimes and nickels they had earned.

"Splendid, splendid." Mr. Not So Much nodded with approval to see the money they had earned. However, his approval lessened somewhat when he heard that the money was to be spent on poem books, ice cream, candy, and fur coats. He was not sure what the world was coming to. Spend, spend, spend. A fool and his money are soon parted, he thought. Shaking his head and stroking his chin, he went on his way — leaving the Ten O'Clock Club with no further business of the day than to adjourn their meeting.

"We will close the meeting by reciting our pledge," Elsie May said, nudging Little Ann, who got up from the grass and stood beside the others and tried to say the pledge with them as best she could.

"I pledge to be a loyal member of the Ten O'Clock Club, and to obey its rules and keep its secrets forever and ever."

"Meeting dismissed," said Elsie May.